Stock and Rocket

Published in 2018
by Stock and Rocket, an imprint of
Igloo Books Ltd, Cottage Farm
Sywell, NN6 0BJ
www.igloobooks.com

FIR003 1118
2 4 6 8 10 9 7 5 3 1
ISBN 978-1-78905-286-2

© iStock / Getty Images
Written by Joff Brown
Illustrated by Chris Chatterton

Printed and manufactured in China

This book belongs to:

....

Night-time Ninja

"It's seven o'clock, George!" called Dad. "Time for bed."
"I'm not tired," said George. "No bed for me tonight. I'm the
bedtime buccaneer!" he cried, running into the kitchen.

"You'll never catch me!" cried George, diving under the table.
Dad came in and looked all around. "Where are you, George?" he asked.

Dad didn't see George creep quietly out from
under the table and into the living room.

"Come on, George," said Dad, patiently. "Where are you?" Just then, from behind the dusty curtains, there was a loud, ATISHOO!

"There you are!" cried Dad, just as George rushed out of the room and dashed upstairs, laughing. "Not tired! Not tired!" cried George.

Upstairs, Dad heard a noise from George's bedroom.

"I'm in here!" called George. "Can you find me?"

"I know where you are," said Dad, pulling open the wardrobe door.

"Got you!" cried Dad. Except it wasn't George at all. It was his big, old teddy, dressed in a pair of old pyjamas.

"Nice try, Dad," said George, slipping out from under the bed and dashing out of the room. "No one can catch the night-time ninja."

"It's time to put my secret plan into action," thought Dad. He went downstairs to the kitchen and rummaged in the fridge.

Hearing the noise, George crept down to see what was going on, but he couldn't find Dad anywhere.

Puzzled, George crept carefully up to his bedroom.

On the bedside table, there were some milk and cookies.

"Even ninjas need a snack," thought George, as he climbed into bed.

Suddenly, Dad sprang out of the darkness. "It's a trap," he laughed. "You may be the night-time ninja, but I'm the pyjama police." "Caught at last," said George. "I guess it really is time for bed after all."

The Cake Snatcher

It was the morning of Jed's birthday party.

Dad had baked a big birthday cake, oozing with jam and cream.

"Can we try it?" asked Jed and his little sister, Kayley.

But Dad said they had to wait until the party.

"Aww," said Kayley, as she and Jed went upstairs, "I want a piece, NOW!"

"I've got a plan," said Jed. He put on a red cape and black mask.

"This is a job for... the Cake Snatcher and his sidekick, the Cupcake Kid."

The Cake Snatcher
and the Cupcake Kid
plotted and schemed,
until they had a truly
dastardly plan.

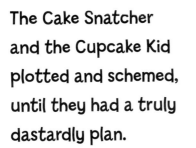

The Cupcake Kid lowered
a doll on a string out of
the bedroom window,
until it tapped on the
kitchen window.

"What's that sound?" asked Dad. The doll tapped against the window and as Dad turned around, it shot upwards. "I'd better take a look," said Dad, going out into the garden.

While Dad was outside, the Cake Snatcher sneaked into the kitchen.

The Cake Snatcher had forgotten about Jango, their shaggy, old dog, who began to bark. "Shh, boy," hissed the Cake Snatcher.

He saw a plate of sausages and quickly gave it to Jango, who happily ate a few, then went back to sleep.

Just then, the Cupcake Kid joined the Cake Snatcher.
Together, they reached for the cake, when suddenly a voice boomed
out. "Not so fast, I'm Super-Dad! I saw the doll and figured out your
plan. You two super-villains are in big trouble."

Jed and Kayley took off their masks. "What's going to happen?" they asked.
"Your punishment is that you have to help me ice this cake. If you make up
for your dastardly deeds, you can get the first two slices at the party."
"Thanks, Dad!" said Jed. "That sounds like a good plan."

So, Jed and Kayley helped Dad to ice and decorate the cake.
They all agreed that it was going to be a fantastic birthday treat
and definitely worth waiting for!